Monster Chef

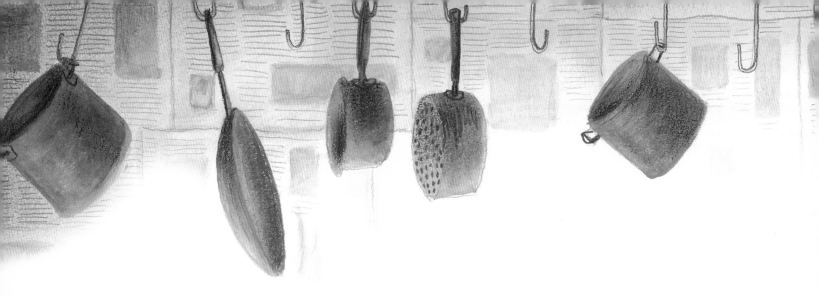

For the kids of Wagait Beach and Belyuen—NB

Scholastic Canada Ltd.
604 King Street West, Toronto, Ontario M5V 1E1, Canada

Scholastic Inc.
557 Broadway, New York, NY 10012, USA

Scholastic Australia Pty Limited
PO Box 579, Gosford, NSW 2250, Australia

Scholastic New Zealand Limited
Private Bag 94407, Botany, Manukau 2163, New Zealand

Scholastic Children's Books
Euston House, 24 Eversholt Street, London NW1 1DB, UK

www.scholastic.ca

Nick used watercolour, gouache, pencil and pastel to create these illustrations.

Library and Archives Canada Cataloguing in Publication
Bland, Nick, 1973-, author, illustrator
Monster chef / written and illustrated by Nick Bland.
ISBN 978-1-4431-2881-0 (bound).--ISBN 978-1-4431-2882-7 (pbk.)
I. Title.
PZ7.B557Mo 2014   j823'.92   C2013-907833-9

First published by Scholastic Australia in 2014.
This edition published by Scholastic Canada Ltd. in 2014.

6 5 4 3 2 1   Printed in Malaysia 108   14 15 16 17 18

Monster Chef

Nick Bland

Scholastic Canada Ltd.
Toronto New York London Auckland Sydney
Mexico City New Delhi Hong Kong Buenos Aires

Marcel was a monster of medium size,
with crotchety horns and googly eyes.
Like most other monsters, he worked every night,
giving the neighbourhood children a fright.

His climbing was perfect . . .

his creeping was good . . .

and he hid very well,
just like all monsters should.

He was lumpy and grumpy and suitably hairy,
but Marcel had a problem . . .

BOO!

He just wasn't scary.

Night after night, whatever he did,
he couldn't scare a single kid.

He couldn't scare Abbie.

He couldn't scare Bob.

He was totally hopeless at doing his job.

But when he came home at the end of the night,
a smile crossed his face as he flicked on the light.
He kicked off his shoes, hung his hat on a hook,

went into the kitchen . . .

and started to cook!

He stirred and
he poured
and he plucked
with delight,
forgetting entirely
his horrible night.

He baked and he sizzled, he fried and he boiled,
with anything rotten
      or crawling
            or spoiled.

He made earthworm spaghetti and hot cactus pies,
with smelly-sock soup and a cockroach surprise.

There were rotten bananas on apple-core cake,
and a dollop of sludge on a beetle-shell bake.

From each perfect dish he took one little bite,
and saved all the rest for the following night.

And when it grew dark, Marcel went to work,
looking for suitable places to lurk.

He climbed through a window
and quietly hid.

Then the door slowly opened
and in rode a kid.
He hopped off his trike
and he pulled out the chair . . .

"OH NO!"
thought Marcel,
"MY DINNER'S UP THERE!"

But Marcel was too late.
His food had been seen.
The brave-looking kid
had turned totally green!

He screamed
and he ran away
into the night.
And that's how
Marcel gave his
very first fright.

So he
horrified
Abbie

...and he terrified Bob.

Marcel, at long last, could take pride in his job!

Now he's opened a restaurant called

MONSTER'S DELIGHT.

Where he still gets to give the occasional fright.

And for those who are snarling
or snorting their snouts,

he cooks just for them . . .